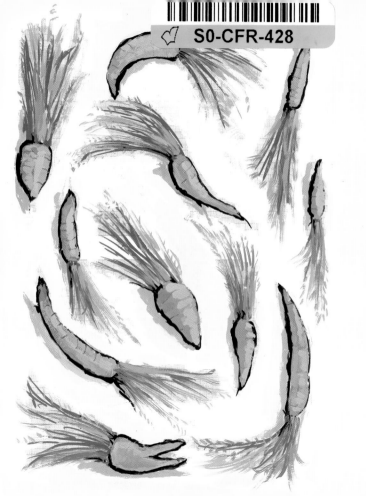

All inquiries should be addressed to
Barron's Educational Series, Inc
250 Wireless Boulevard
Hauppauge, NY 1178

http://www.barronseduc.com

International Standard Book No. 0-7641-5543-
Library of Congress Catalog Card No. 200109805!

Printed in Chin

9 8 7 6 5 4 3 2

Flop-Ear

Guido Van Genechten

Rabbits come in all shapes and sizes.
There are big rabbits and little rabbits,
fat rabbits and thin rabbits,
girl rabbits and boy rabbits.
And they all have two long ears.
Flop-Ear had two long ears, too, only...

Flop-Ear's were different.

All the other rabbits had ears that stood straight up.
But Flop-Ear's right ear hung down.
"Lop-ear Flop-Ear!"
they shouted at him.
"Why can't you
stick your ear up like us?"

Flop-Ear longed to have two straight ears,
but how? When he hung upside down,
his ears were quite straight, but he couldn't
spend all his life like that...

Flop-Ear tried hiding his ears under his grandma's
lamp shade. It was hot
and uncomfortable,
and the other rabbits
laughed at him.

Flop-Ear propped his ear up with a carrot.

He tied it to a stick with some string.

He wrapped his ear in a big bandage.

He tried a clothespin
on the end of his dad's
fishing rod.

He even held his ear up
with a balloon.

The other rabbits were laughing so much they nearly cried.

Poor Flop-Ear. Nothing seemed to work. By now he was very sad: "I'll just have to cut my ear off. And I never, ever want to see those rabbits again!"

Flop-Ear sat down all by himself and cried.

The next day, Flop-Ear went to the doctor.

The doctor examined both his ears.
"Mmm...," he said, "you know,
there's really nothing wrong with
that ear; it hears perfectly well.
Besides, all ears are different.
Here, have a nice carrot.
They're good for you!"

On his way home, Flop-Ear thought about what the
doctor had said. It was true, all ears were different.
"It's just that I have two different ears, one standing
up and one lying down."

Flop-Ear laughed at himself. One up, one down!
He felt much happier. The other rabbits
saw him coming. They shouted out:
"Hey, here's Flop-Ear!"
They were all so pleased
to see him.

Soon, all the rabbits were tying carrots to their ears — one ear up and one ear down. What fun they all had — and they were...

ALL THE SAME!

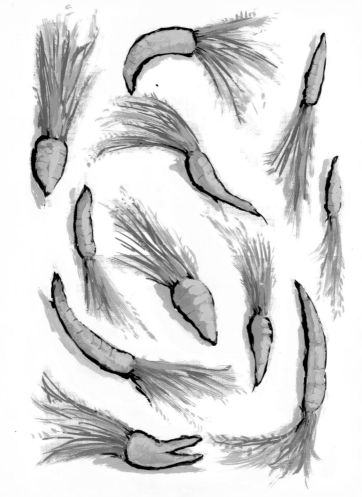